HOPSCOTCH
FAIRY TALES

The Elves
and the
Shoemaker

Retold by Anne Walter

Illustrated by Andy Rowland

FRANKLIN WATTS
LONDON•SYDNEY

First published in 2009 by
Franklin Watts
338 Euston Road
London
NW1 3BH

Franklin Watts Australia
Level 17/207 Kent Street
Sydney
NSW 2000

Text © Anne Walter 2009
Illustrations © Andy Rowland 2009

A CIP catalogue record for this book is available
from the British Library.

ISBN 978 0 7496 8537 9 (hbk)
ISBN 978 0 7496 8543 0 (pbk)

Series Editor: Melanie Palmer
Series Advisor: Dr Barrie Wade
Series Designer: Peter Scoulding

Printed in China

Franklin Watts is a division of
Hachette Children's Books,
an Hachette UK company
www.hachette.co.uk

Once in a little town there lived
a shoemaker and his wife.

They made lots of shoes, but they were still very poor. One day, the shoemaker had just one piece of leather left.

"There's not enough money for any more leather to make shoes," said his wife.

Sadly, the shoemaker left the last piece of leather out on the table and went to bed.

But when he woke up the next
morning, the leather had gone. In
its place were two beautiful boots.

The shoemaker was amazed. "Who could have made these boots?" he wondered.

As soon as the shoemaker opened his shop, a man came in and bought the boots.

"They're such lovely boots, I'll give you double the price," said the man, smiling.

"That's enough to buy leather for two more pairs of shoes!" said the shoemaker's wife.

That night, the shoemaker and his wife went to bed and put the new leather on the table.

Again, when they woke up,
the leather had gone. This time,
they saw two pairs of shiny shoes.

The shoemaker was amazed.

"This is incredible!" he said.

"What pretty shoes!" said his wife.

When the shoemaker opened
his shop, he sold the shoes
straight away.

"Now we have enough money to make three more pairs of shoes," said the shoemaker's wife.

That night, the shoemaker and
his wife did not go to sleep. Instead
they hid and waited to see what
would happen.

Suddenly they heard two little
voices laughing. Then two elves
jumped out and started to make
shoes from the new leather!

The shoemaker and his wife gasped. The little elves looked happy, but they had bare feet and were dressed in rags.

"I've got an idea," whispered his wife. "Let's make new shoes and new suits for them."

The next day, the couple put
two pairs of boots and two little
suits out as well as the leather.

22

The little elves jumped out as soon
as the lights were off. They saw the
new clothes and giggled in delight!

Instead of making shoes,
the elves put on the new clothes.
Then they skipped away.

This time the leather was still on the table when the shoemaker and his wife woke up. Only the little suits and little boots had gone.

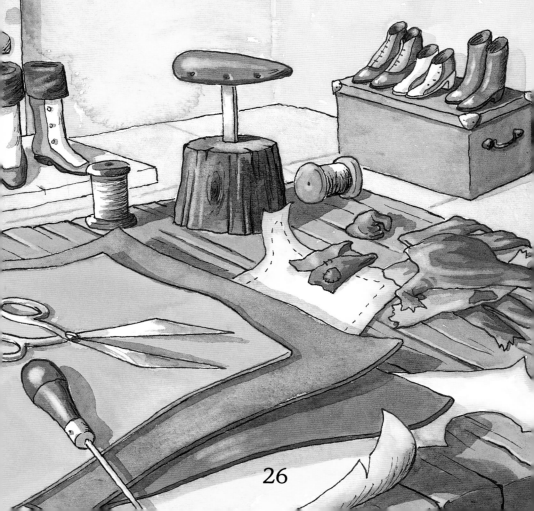

The shoemaker and his wife were still happy. Their shoes were now so popular that they never worried about money again.

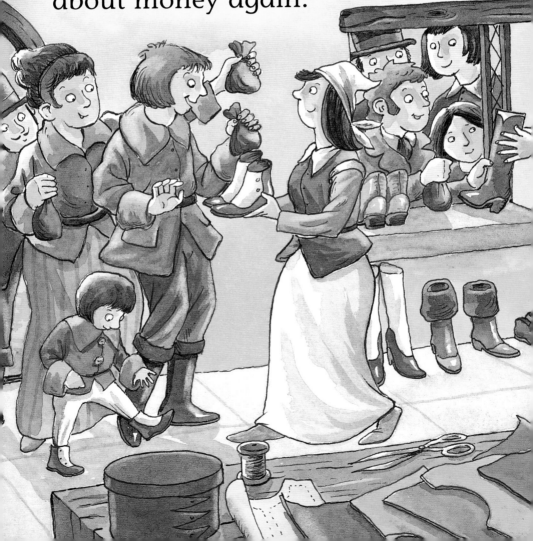

They also never forgot
about their little helpers.

Puzzle 1

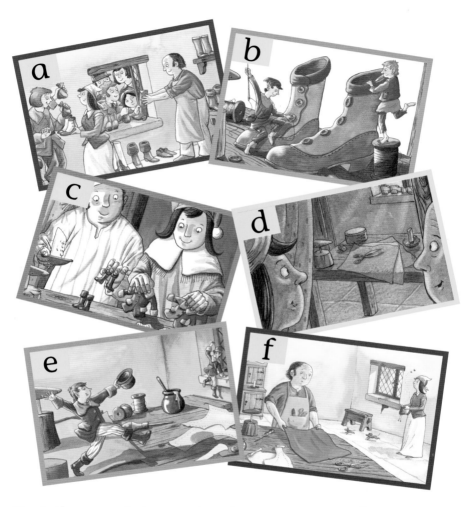

Put these pictures in the correct order.

Which event do you think is most important?

Now try writing the story in your own words!

Puzzle 2

1. I make shoes all day long.

2. It's fun being small!

3. My purse is empty.

4. I need to buy more leather.

5. My shop is full today!

6. We like working at night.

Choose the correct speech bubbles for each character. Can you think of any others? Turn over to find the answers.

Answers

Puzzle 1

The correct order is: 1f, 2d, 3b ,4c, 5e, 6a.

Puzzle 2

The shoemaker: 1, 5

The shoemaker's wife: 3, 4

The elves: 2, 6

Look out for more Hopscotch Fairy Tales:

The Emperor's New Clothes
ISBN 978 0 7496 7421 2

Cinderella
ISBN 978 0 7496 7417 5

Jack and the Beanstalk
ISBN 978 0 7496 7422 9

The Pied Piper of Hamelin
ISBN 978 0 7496 7419 9

Snow White
ISBN 978 0 7496 7418 2

The Three Billy Goats Gruff
ISBN 978 0 7496 7420 5

Hansel and Gretel
ISBN 978 0 7496 7904 0

Little Red Riding Hood
ISBN 978 0 7496 7907 1

Rapunzel
ISBN 978 0 749 67906 4

Rumpelstiltskin
ISBN 978 0 7496 7908 8

The Three Little Pigs
ISBN 978 0 7496 7905 7

Goldilocks and the Three Bears
ISBN 978 0 7496 7903 3

For more Hopscotch books go to: www.franklinwatts.co.uk